FAMILY

FAMILY

by Isabell Monk
illustrated by Janice Lee Porter

Carolrhoda Books, Inc./Minneapolis

The drops of rain looked like falling stars as Mama, Papa, and I drove to Aunt Poogee's farm. We rolled down our windows and took in the sweet country air. The rain on the dusty road smelled so good! "Smells good enough to eat!" Aunt Poogee would say.

"Aunt Poogee," I squealed as Papa stopped the car. I ran to her with hugs and kisses.

Mama hugged her so long and so hard that Aunt Poogee began to rock her like a baby. "Oh, Evie," Aunt Poogee said. Then she turned to Papa. "Come on over here, David, and give me some sugar," she teased. And she hugged him, too.

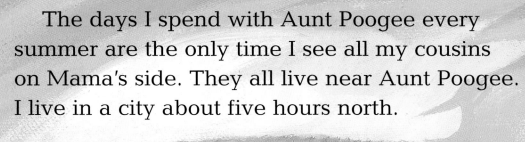

The days I spend with Aunt Poogee every summer are the only time I see all my cousins on Mama's side. They all live near Aunt Poogee. I live in a city about five hours north.

My surprise was in the back seat. I ran back to the car. I carried it inside and found…

…Aunt Mil, Uncle Thomas, Michael, and Gregory.

Michael plays the trumpet. All the time.

Gregory is wild. Aunt Poogee says, "That boy likes to stir things up."

I carried my box into
the kitchen. There were...

...Aunt Frances and Uncle Sid, unpacking the picnic basket they had brought.

All their kids were helping: Jackie, Celestine,
Bobby, little Paul, Kay, and Yvonne. Kay handed
little Paul to Bobby.

The back door opened and...

...Uncle Tuney walked in. He handed each of us a "cabbage leaf"—a nice green one dollar bill. He was holding a catfish he had caught. It looked just like him.

Gregory bounced into the kitchen.
He looked inside my box.

"What's that?" he asked.

"It's for dessert," I said.

"Pickles?" he asked.

Jackie and Kay looked at me. I just nodded yes.

Then Gregory said, "That's different. But come to think of it, so are you."

"Oh, what do you know, Gregory?" Jackie asked.

Gregory didn't even hear her. "Come on everybody," he shouted. We followed him outside.

The rain had stopped. The silk-soft grass on the hill was my favorite color of green, "Asparagus," from my big box of crayons.

Gregory always had us play school bus. He was the driver. When I started to climb on the bus, he said, "Hey, I thought city girls rode in taxis!" But he let me on. Michael blew a blast on his trumpet.

Gregory drove us to the pigpen. The piglets, Nikki and Nelson, kind of barked at us as we rolled by. At the chicken coop, we said hello to Henry, the rooster, and Elnora, Viola, and Tiny, the hens.

Gregory drove us past Uncle Tuney grilling the catfish. We got off and on the bus as Gregory drove us back down the lane.

"It's time to crank the ice cream!" Aunt Poogee called. The school bus disappeared. We all raced to the big wraparound porch and took turns cranking the real vanilla ice cream.

When we carried the ice cream inside, I heard
Mama say, "This is enough food to last us a month!"

Everyone had brought their specialty. Aunt Poogee's hot homemade rolls were under white tea towels. You didn't even have to chew them—they just melted in your mouth. Uncle Tuney's catfish was on a big platter. Aunt Frances had brought her family recipe corn pudding.

There were fresh greens, potato salad, sliced tomatoes, sliced cucumbers, fresh corn on the cob, barbequed chicken, crab cakes, and Aunt Poogee's family recipe lemonade. Everything except the crab in the crab cakes and the lemons in the lemonade came from right here on Aunt Poogee's farm.

"You people look like you haven't had a decent meal since last August," said Aunt Poogee. "Who's gonna say grace?"

Gregory said, "I will." As we bowed our heads, we heard him say, "Good greens, good meat, good grief, let's eat!"

There were a few chuckles before Celestine said, "May we continue to be blessed with good times, good food, and loving family." With that everybody said an "Amen."

We ate, talked, and laughed a lot.

When it was time for dessert, Mama brought out the homemade ice cream. Aunt Mil sliced the coconut cake. Aunt Poogee went back for my pickles. "Hope brought a surprise," she announced.

Everyone looked at the plate of big, bumpy, green pickles. There was silence.

"My cousin Laura on my papa's side taught me
how to make this," I said.
Gregory picked up a pickle. He sniffed it.
"Go ahead Gregory," Aunt Poogee told him.
"It's better than you think."

Gregory took a big bite. Then he said,
"Yum!"

Yvonne bit into a pickle. "Hey," she
said, "there's a peppermint stick inside.
De-licious!"

Everybody else started
eating pickles, too.

After supper, the grown-ups cleaned up while my cousins played checkers and crazy eights.

Aunt Poogee and I sat on the porch swing. I saw a bat fly across the buttery moon.

"A penny for your thoughts," Aunt Poogee cooed. Her voice was like a lullaby.

"Everything we ate tonight was a family recipe," I said.

"Yes, everything," Aunt Poogee said. "Our family recipes now include Hope's Peppermint Pickles!"

I felt proud.

We floated on the porch swing, listening to the crickets and frogs.

"Sharing food is a good way of sharing family," Aunt Poogee said. "Always add a cup of tradition from your papa's family to a cup from your mama's side."

She nuzzled my neck. The nuzzling made me giggle.

"You forgot one thing, Aunt Poogee," I said.

"What's that, Baby?" she asked.

"Add lots and lots of love!"

"Sounds like a good recipe," Aunt Poogee laughed.

"It's a recipe for a family," I said. "Mine."

AUNT MIL'S COCONUT CAKE

1/2 cup butter or shortening
1 cup sugar
2 eggs, separated
2 cups cake flour
1/4 tsp. salt

1 tsp. ground cinnamon
1 tsp. ground ginger
2-1/2 tsp. baking powder
2/3 cup whole milk
1 tsp. pure vanilla extract

Preheat oven to 350°. Cream butter and sugar together, adding sugar gradually. Beat until fluffy. Stir in beaten egg yolks. Mix dry ingredients together and add them alternately with milk and vanilla to creamed mixture. Fold in stiffly beaten egg whites. Grease and flour two 8- or 9-inch cake pans. Add batter and bake for 20 minutes.

Let cool then
add frositng.

FROSTING

2 tbls. milk or water or pineapple juice
1 cup confectioners' sugar
1/2 tsp. pure vanilla extract
10–12 oz. shredded coconut

Stir the sugar gradually into the milk or water or juice. Add vanilla. Add more sugar if the frosting is not thick enough. Frost bottom layer completely and top with about half of the coconut. Then add top layer, frost, and sprinkle with the rest of the coconut.

AUNT POOGEE'S LEMONADE

6 lemons
2 limes
6 cups warm water
2/3 to 1 cup sugar

Squeeze the juice of the lemons and the limes and mix with the warm water and sugar. Make sure the sugar is well dissolved. Serve chilled or over ice.

AUNT FRANCES'S CORN PUDDIN'

1 pkg. corn muffin mix
1 stick butter or margarine, cut up
1 15-1/2 oz. can whole kernel corn with juice
1 15-1/2 oz. can creamed corn
16 oz. sour cream
(optional: 1/4 tsp. sugar, 1 tsp. nutmeg, and 1 tsp. cinnamon)

Preheat oven to 350°. Stir all ingredients together in a soufflé box or deep dish and bake for 1 hour. Serve warm.

HOPE'S SWEET AND SOUR PICKLES

1 jar of whole sour pickles
1 box of peppermint sticks
(1 plastic straw or a chopstick)

Take pickle from jar. Make a hole in the pickle from end to end with a plastic straw or a chopstick. Place peppermint stick in hole and eat.

To Henry Monk and All My Family—I.M.

To Isabell with love—J.L.P.

Carolrhoda Books, Inc.
A division of Lerner Publishing Group
241 First Avenue North
Minneapolis, MN 55401 U.S.A.

Website address: www.carolrhodabooks.com

The Library of Congress has cataloged an earlier hardcover edition as follows:

Monk, Isabell.
     Family / by Isabell Monk ; illustrations by Janice Lee Porter.
        p.   cm.
     Summary: Hope's new and unusual dessert blends well with the traditional dishes prepared by her cousins and Aunt Poogee at their annual summer get-together.
     ISBN: 1–57505–485–X (lib. bdg. : alk. paper)
     [1. Family life—Fiction. 2. Food—Fiction.] I. Porter, Janice Lee, ill. II. Title.
PZ7.M75115 Fam 2001
[E]—dc21   00-009398

Manufactured in the United States of America
3 4 5 6 7 8 – JR – 10 09 08 07 06 05